LUCY DANIELS
Cat Crazy

Illustrated by Paul Howard

*Hodder
Children's
Books*

a division of Hodder Headline plc

Special thanks to Narinder Dhami

Text copyright © 1998 Ben M. Baglio
Created by Ben M. Baglio, London W12 7QY
Illustrations copyright © 1998 Paul Howard
Cover illustration by Chris Chapman

First published in Great Britain in 1998
by Hodder Children's Books

A Catalogue record for this book is available from the British Library

ISBN 0 340 71375 5

Typeset by Avon Dataset Ltd, Bidford-on-Avon, Warks

Printed and bound in Great Britain by
Mackays of Chatham plc, Chatham, Kent

Hodder Children's Books
a division of Hodder Headline plc
338 Euston Road
London NW1 3BH

Contents

To Billy, a very special kitten, much missed.

1

A picnic by the river

"Mandy Hope, I shouldn't think you can eat one more thing!" laughed Mrs Hope, as Mandy opened the cake tin. "You and James have both eaten enough to feed an army!"

Mandy grinned at her mother. "I was just wondering if there were any of those raisin scones left," she said.

"Can I have one too, please?" asked James eagerly. He was lying on the picnic blanket, with his Labrador puppy, Blackie, curled up beside him.

"There's just one." Mandy held up the scone. "We'll share it."

Blackie woofed hopefully.

"OK, Blackie." Mandy smiled at the puppy, who was wagging his tail like a little black flag. "We'll all share it!"

Mr Hope shook his head. "I've never seen two children and one young dog eat quite so much in my life!" he said to Mrs Hope.

"I always seem to get hungrier on holiday!" said James with a grin. "And so does Blackie!"

The Hopes, Mandy's best friend, James Hunter, and, of course, Blackie, were on holiday for two weeks in an area of the Gloucestershire countryside called the Cotswolds. Mandy and James hadn't been to the Cotswolds before, and they were enjoying walking and cycling around the gently rolling hills and valleys. They weren't staying in one place, but were driving to a different pretty Cotswold village every few days.

Yesterday they had arrived at their last stop, a small bed-and-breakfast hotel in a village called Bilbury. Today was Wednesday, and Mandy and James were determined to make the most of the last few days of the holiday, before they went home on Sunday morning.

"I think this is the best holiday I've ever had," Mandy said happily, as she fed Blackie a tiny piece of scone. "I'm so glad we came!"

"I'm really glad you asked Blackie and me

to come too," said James. "Blackie's been quite good, hasn't he?"

They all looked at Blackie, who was sitting very still and staring hopefully at the scone Mandy was eating.

"He always is when there's food around!" Mandy laughed. She loved being on holiday with James and his dog. It was almost as good as having a pet of her own.

Mandy's parents were both vets, and worked in a surgery built on to the back of their house in the village of Welford. Because the surgery was always so busy with other people's animals, Mandy couldn't have a pet of her own, and it was difficult for Mr and Mrs Hope to take a holiday. But this time they'd managed to find another vet, Alison Morgan, to stand in for them.

"Wouldn't it be great if we could have brought all the animals from Animal Ark on holiday with us?" said Mandy with a grin. "I wonder how they all are?"

Mr Hope laughed. "I don't think there would have been room in the car for the rest of us!"

Mrs Hope put her arm round Mandy. "We'll ring Alison tonight, and find out how everyone is getting on," she promised.

James grinned. "Mandy doesn't forget about animals even on holiday."

"Of course I don't!" said Mandy. "And talking of animals, it's about time we took Blackie for a walk."

Blackie opened his eyes, and pricked up his ears at the word "walk".

James jumped up. "All right," he said. "But I've eaten so much, I can hardly move!"

"You'd better keep Blackie on his lead," said Mr Hope. "We don't want him taking a dip in the river."

Mandy bent down, and clipped the lead firmly to Blackie's collar. "We'd never get him out again!" she said. Although she and James had been trying to train Blackie for months, he still didn't always do as he was told. "Ready, James?"

James nodded.

"Don't be too long," Mrs Hope called after them, as they set off along the river-bank.

5

"Look, James!" Mandy said, pointing at the water. "Aren't the dragonflies beautiful?"

They stopped to watch the dragonflies skimming over the surface of the river for a few minutes. But Blackie was soon tugging at the lead, so they walked on.

Mandy smiled. She loved having Blackie around, and James didn't mind sharing him at all. She bent down to stroke the puppy, then handed the lead to James. "Here, it's your turn."

"Maybe we'd better go back now," said James, winding Blackie's lead firmly round his hand. "Your mum said not to go too far."

"Lazybones!" Mandy teased him. "We'll just go round the next bend of the river. Then we'll turn back."

James nodded. "OK. But next time we have a picnic, remind me not to eat so much!"

They carried on along the bank. The river twisted and turned in a long curve, and Mandy and James followed its path.

There were some ducks swimming in the

water, and Blackie began to bark as soon as he spotted them. The ducks swam off as fast as they could.

"He won't hurt you," James called. "He just wants to make friends, that's all." He turned to Mandy with a grin, as the ducks scuttled off in all directions. "I don't think they believe me!"

But Mandy wasn't listening. She grabbed James's arm, and pointed at something ahead of them. "Look, James!"

There was a black cat sitting on the river-bank. It was having a wash, and licking its leg with its pink tongue.

"Hello, puss!" said James, as the cat stopped washing, and stared curiously at them.

"Isn't it gorgeous!" Mandy said. "Let's go and make friends."

"What about Blackie?" James asked, looking down at his puppy, who was sniffing around in the grass. "It might not like dogs."

Just then Blackie noticed the cat, and pricked up his ears. He was used to cats, because James had one called Benji, but he always got excited when he saw one. He started barking loudly. The black cat looked alarmed, and jumped to its feet.

"Quiet, Blackie!" James gasped, trying to stop himself from being dragged along the river-bank. "You'll frighten it!"

Mandy frowned. "Look, James," she said in a worried voice. "I think it's hurt!"

James stared at the little black cat. He could see what Mandy meant. One of its front legs didn't look quite right. The cat was holding it awkwardly across the other one, so that its front paws were crossed. "What's wrong with it?" he asked anxiously.

Mandy was staring hard at the cat. "I don't know," she said. "But we can't just leave it here if it's hurt."

Mandy began to walk slowly towards the cat, holding her hand out in front of her. The cat watched her with big green eyes. It didn't look scared at all. It started to walk towards her, limping heavily on its front leg.

Quickly Mandy knelt down, and held out her hand close to the cat's face. For a moment, the cat didn't do anything. Then

it sniffed Mandy's hand, and let her stroke its head.

"Can you see what's wrong with its leg?" James called. He tied Blackie to a nearby tree, and went over to stroke the cat himself. "Do you think it was hit by a car?"

Mandy shook her head. "There's no blood," she said, puzzled. "I think it may be an old injury."

"You mean it was hurt somehow, and left with a limp?" James looked upset. "That's awful."

"I wonder where it's come from," Mandy said, tickling the little cat's tummy. "Maybe it lives in the village."

They could just see the village where they were staying, through the trees that grew along the river-bank. But it seemed a very long way for a little cat with a bad leg to walk.

Mandy looked worried. "I hope it isn't lost," she said.

"Maybe we ought to take it back to your mum and dad," James suggested. But, right at that moment, the little cat got up, and started to limp away in the other direction.

"We'd better follow, and make sure it's all right," Mandy decided quickly.

James went to get Blackie, and they all hurried after the little cat. The cat looked over its shoulder and saw them following, but didn't seem to mind.

"We'd better not go too far," James said nervously. "Your mum and dad will be wondering where we are."

Mandy didn't answer. Instead she nudged James in the ribs, and pointed down the river-bank.

"Wow!" she gasped. "Look at that!"

2

The Puss-in-Boat

"It's a boat full of cats!" said James, his eyes wide with amazement.

The boat was a long, thin barge, the kind of boat that people sometimes live in, instead of a house. It was painted in reds and blues, and there was a picture of a black-and-white cat painted on the side. Above that, the name of the boat was written in red letters — *The Puss-in-Boat.*

There was a coal-black cat, a marmalade cat and a tabby cat asleep on top of the cabin, all curled up together. Two black-and-white cats were eating from food bowls on the boat deck, and Mandy and James counted another six cats walking up and down, or sitting washing themselves. As they stared in amazement, the little black cat jumped gracefully from the river-bank on to the deck. Then she sat down to have another wash.

"*The Puss-in-Boat,*" said James, with a grin. "I can see why it's called that!"

"Me too!" Mandy agreed, her eyes shining. She'd never seen so many cats all together in one place before. "Let's go a bit closer."

Mandy, James and Blackie hurried along the river-bank until they reached the barge. As they got closer, they could see that the boat was quite shabby, and needed a new coat of paint. But there were pots of flowers on the deck, and all the cats looked healthy and well fed.

"How many cats are there?" James asked in a dazed voice.

"Well, I can see twelve," said Mandy, as a big orange-and-white cat padded round from the other side of the boat. "No, thirteen."

"Did you count the grey one near the flowers?" James asked, pointing it out.

Mandy couldn't remember, so they had to start counting all over again. Meanwhile, the little black cat was sniffing round the empty food bowls. When she realised there was no food left, she began to miaow loudly.

"Who looks after all these cats?" James wondered.

Mandy was still counting under her breath. "Oh no, now I've lost count again!" she sighed. "How many do you make it, James?"

"Eighteen," said someone else's voice.

A fair-haired boy of about Mandy's age had appeared from below the deck, and was smiling shyly at them. Mandy and James smiled back.

"Come on board and say hello to our

cats," the boy said. "Mum won't mind, will you, Mum?"

A young woman in denim dungarees, with the same colour hair as the boy, followed him on to the deck. She waved at Mandy and James. "Hello. I'm Lucy Browne, and this is my son, Martin. Do you like cats?"

"We're Mandy Hope and James Hunter," Mandy said, "and we love cats."

"Well, do come and meet ours. We're always looking for volunteers to give them a cuddle." Lucy grinned at them. "It isn't easy finding the time to give eighteen cats all the love and attention they need!"

Mandy and James were thrilled. James tied Blackie to the nearest tree, and they stepped on to the barge. Blackie looked a bit disappointed for a moment. Then he lay down, put his nose between his paws and went to sleep.

As soon as Mandy and James were aboard, they were surrounded by cats. Mandy scooped up the nearest one into her arms, and he snuggled down on her shoulder. He

was a big marmalade cat, and he had the loudest purr Mandy had ever heard.

"That's Pusskin," said Lucy. "He's our oldest cat. He's fifteen."

Mandy gave Pusskin a cuddle. He purred even louder, and put his paws round her neck. Mandy didn't want to put him down, but there were so many other cats begging for attention that she had to. She knelt down and stroked as many as she could, trying hard to remember all their names.

James was holding a beautiful tabby, with big green eyes and an orange mark on her forehead. "What's this one called?" he asked.

"That's Penny," said Martin. "She catches anything that moves."

"And leaves it on the deck for us to trip over next morning!" added Lucy.

"Why do you have so many cats?" Mandy asked curiously, stroking Lily, a black cat with glossy fur.

"Well, first of all, we had three cats of our own," Lucy began. "Then we took in a few strays, and people started bringing us more and more," she explained. "Three of the cats were left homeless when their elderly owners died. I hadn't got the heart to turn any of them away."

"Some of them have been badly treated," said Martin. He pointed to a very strange-looking cat who was asleep in a shady corner of the deck. "Like Muffin."

"Poor thing," said James. "He looks as if most of his fur has been shaved off."

"The vet had to do that," said Lucy. "Muffin's a Persian cat, and their fur has to be brushed regularly or it gets all tangled up."

"You mean his owner didn't look after him properly?" Mandy asked indignantly. She hated it when people couldn't be bothered to look after their pets.

Lucy nodded. "Muffin's fur was such a mess, we couldn't brush it," she said. "But it'll grow back."

There was suddenly a loud *miaow* behind them. They all jumped, and turned round. The little black cat was still sitting by the empty food bowl.

Lucy laughed. "I think you've met Queenie, haven't you?"

"Yes." Mandy knelt down, and stroked her. "She's gorgeous! But what happened to her leg?"

"She got knocked down by a car," said Lucy. "And her owner didn't want her back, because her leg never healed properly."

"That's terrible!" said Mandy.

Queenie miaowed again at the top of her voice, and Lucy covered her ears. "She won't stop until we feed her." She laughed.

"I'll feed her," Martin offered. "I think Effie needs feeding too."

"Who's Effie?" James asked.

Lucy smiled. "She's the newest addition to our family – and she produced four babies almost as soon as she arrived here!"

"Kittens!" said Mandy, her face lighting up. "Where are they?"

"Below deck," said Martin, pointing at the cabin door.

"All tucked up in a basket with their mum!" Lucy added. "They're only three weeks old."

"Where did Effie come from?" James asked.

"Mrs Cox, who runs the village post office, found her wandering about, and brought her to us," Lucy explained. "She would have loved to keep the cat herself, but she's got a couple of dogs already."

"And we've taken in a couple of other cats from the village," Martin added. "Smokey was a stray that old Mr Tilbury brought to us, and Lily belonged to a family who were going to live abroad and couldn't take her with them."

"Can we see the kittens now?" Mandy asked eagerly.

"Of course, if you have time," said Lucy with a smile.

Mandy and James looked at each other, remembering they'd promised not to be away too long on their walk.

"My mum and dad will be waiting for us just down the river-bank," Mandy said reluctantly. She was longing to see the kittens, and there were still some cats she hadn't said hello to yet, but they couldn't keep her parents waiting much longer.

"Well, why don't you ask them if they'd like to come to *The Puss-in-Boat* for a cup of tea?" suggested Lucy. "Then they can meet the cats, and the kittens too."

Mandy's eyes lit up. "That would be brilliant!" she said. "Come on, James. Let's go and tell them."

Mandy and James stepped over the cats still milling around their feet, and climbed off the barge.

"We'll be back soon, we hope!" Mandy called, waving at their new friends. James untied Blackie, and then the three of them ran back along the river-bank the way they'd come.

"There you are!" said Mrs Hope, as Mandy, James and Blackie raced up to them. "We were beginning to wonder where you were."

"Oh, we've had a brilliant time!" Mandy gasped. "We went on this barge, and we saw lots of cats!"

"Eighteen cats!" added James. "And Lucy and Martin look after them, and they've invited us all for tea!"

Mr and Mrs Hope looked puzzled. "Could one of you take a deep breath, and go through that again?" asked Mr Hope.

So Mandy told them the whole story.

"It sounds as if Lucy and her son are doing a very good job, looking after all those cats," said Mrs Hope. "We'd love to come and see them."

"Great!" Mandy jumped to her feet. "Can we go right now?"

"Your mum and I had better pack the picnic things away first," said Mr Hope, picking up the basket. "You go on ahead, and tell Lucy and Martin that we're on our way."

"OK!" Mandy and James were already off, running along the river-bank with Blackie bounding along beside them.

"The boat's called *The Puss-in-Boat*," Mandy shouted over her shoulder. "You can't miss it!"

"No, I don't suppose there are many boats with eighteen cats!" Mr Hope called back.

"Aren't Lucy and Martin great?" Mandy said to James, as they raced along the river-bank. "I don't know what would have happened to those cats if they hadn't taken them in."

"I know," James replied. "How can people be so horrible?"

"At least the cats are safe on *The Puss-in-Boat* now," said Mandy.

They followed the bend in the river, and there was the barge, bobbing gently on the water.

"Look, there's Lucy," said James. "She's talking to someone."

Lucy was standing on the river-bank with a man and a woman. As Mandy and James got nearer, they could see that the man's face was red, as if he was cross about something.

"This isn't good enough, young lady," they heard the man say in an angry voice. "I'm going to see to it that all these cats are removed, as soon as I possibly can!"

3

Mr Pengelly

Mandy and James jerked to a halt on the river-bank, and looked at each other in horror. What on earth was going on?

"Mr Pengelly," Lucy was saying politely, "the cats really aren't doing any harm—"

"Well, I found one in my garden the other day, and the day before that!" Mr Pengelly said angrily. He was a small, round man with grey hair and a grey beard. "It's not right keeping so many animals on a boat – it's a health hazard!"

"Why don't you come on to *The Puss-in-Boat* and have a cup of tea?" Lucy suggested. "Then we can have a chat."

Mr Pengelly shook his head. "I'm warning you," he said furiously, "no one in the village wants you here, and we're taking steps to have you moved on! Come along, Marjorie."

Mr Pengelly marched off, and the woman, who hadn't said a word, followed him. Lucy

looked very upset, and so did Martin, who was standing on the barge. James quickly secured Blackie, while Mandy rushed up to Lucy.

"Who were those horrible people?" she asked indignantly.

Lucy sighed. "That's Mr Pengelly and his wife," she said. "They live in the village, and he's been complaining about us ever since we arrived here, five weeks ago."

"Why?" James asked.

"He says the cats are a nuisance, and they go in his garden," Martin replied.

Lucy frowned. "I don't understand it," she said. "Most of the cats are so nervous, they never go as far as the village. They stay close to the boat."

"Doesn't he know you're looking after cats that have been badly treated?" Mandy asked. "Maybe if Mr Pengelly knew that, he might calm down a bit."

Lucy managed a smile. "He never gives me a chance to get a word in edgeways! But I don't think it would make any difference, anyway."

"He wants us to move the boat on somewhere else," added Martin, "but we can't, can we, Mum? The engine needs repairing."

Lucy nodded. "We only just managed to get it this far," she said. "If we're forced to go, we'll have to leave the boat behind and move into a flat, and then, of course, we won't be able to take all the cats with us."

"There must be something we can do," Mandy said desperately. "Maybe we could help you find homes for them."

"We're always trying to find good homes." Martin bent down to stroke Penny. "But most people don't want older cats."

"Well, let's have tea, and we can talk about it later." Lucy smiled at Mandy and James. "Come on to the boat, and I'll put the kettle on."

Mandy and James looked at each other as they followed Lucy on to *The Puss-in-Boat*. If only there was something that she and James could do to help, Mandy thought. But what?

As before, Mandy and James were

surrounded by cats as soon as they reached the deck of the boat. But this time Mandy noticed how many other cats *didn't* come out to be fussed and stroked. There were some who stayed back, hiding themselves away and looking fearfully at Mandy and James. Mandy guessed that these were the animals who had been treated so badly. They were scared of humans they didn't know. What would happen to these cats if Lucy and Martin had to leave *The Puss-in-Boat*?

"Here are your mum and dad, Mandy," said James. In the distance they could see Mr and Mrs Hope walking along the river-bank, carrying the picnic basket.

Mandy turned to Lucy and Martin. "My mum and dad are both vets," she said. "I could ask if they would check over all the cats for you, if you like. If the cats are healthy, then maybe Mr Pengelly won't have so much to complain about."

Lucy's face lit up. "That would be wonderful," she said. "At the moment I have to take the cats to an RSPCA clinic, and it's miles away from here."

Mr and Mrs Hope were getting closer now, so Mandy and James scrambled off the boat, and ran to meet them.

"Dad!" Mandy gasped. "There's this horrible man called Mr Pen-something—"

"Pengelly," said James.

"And he's trying to get rid of *The Puss-in-Boat*!" Mandy continued breathlessly. "And Lucy and Martin might have to move into a flat—"

"And they won't be able to take the cats with them," James finished off.

Mr Hope held up his hand. "Hold on a minute, you two! Let's say hello to your new friends first, before you tell us exactly what's going on."

"Come on then, Dad!" said Mandy eagerly. She grabbed her father's hand, and started tugging him towards the barge, where Lucy and Martin were waving at them.

"Maybe Lucy and Martin would like us to give the cats a quick check-up while we're here," Mrs Hope suggested as they walked up to the boat. "It can't be easy looking after so many cats."

"Oh, thanks, Mum!" said Mandy. "I hoped you'd say that!"

Lucy and Martin were waiting for them on the deck, as they climbed aboard.

"Hello," said Lucy. "Welcome to *The Puss-in-Boat*!"

"Hello." Mrs Hope smiled, as she looked round. "What a wonderful name for a boat full of cats!"

Lucy and Martin looked pleased. For the next few minutes, everyone was busy chatting, and stroking all the cats who curled around their ankles, and jumped up on to their laps.

"Would you like to look round the boat before we have tea?" Lucy asked.

Mandy's eyes lit up. At last she was going to see the kittens!

The Puss-in-Boat wasn't very big, but everything was neat and tidy. Lucy and Martin took their visitors all round the deck, and then to the rooms below. The two bedrooms, kitchen and bathroom were narrow and cramped, but everything was clean.

"Oh, who painted these?" said Mandy. She'd just spotted some water-colour paintings of cats pinned to the cabin walls.

"I did," said Lucy. "I sell them to raise money to look after us and the cats."

"They're lovely!" said Mandy. She pointed to one of the paintings. "That's Pusskin, isn't it?"

"And that's Queenie!" said James. Lucy had painted Queenie, the little black cat with the limp, sitting with her injured leg crossed over the other, just as she'd done when Mandy and James first saw her.

The kittens and their mother were in a basket, under a low, narrow table. Mandy waited impatiently as Lucy knelt down, and gently pulled the basket into view. Five sleepy faces looked up at them. Effie, the mother, was black and white, and so were the kittens, although their markings were all different.

"Oh, they're gorgeous!" Mandy said softly.

Lucy had warned them that Effie was quite a nervous cat, so they all stayed still and quiet, as she lifted the kittens gently out of the basket. She put the biggest one into Mandy's arms.

"This one's called Button," she said. "The others are Candy, Snoopy and Joe."

Even though Button was the biggest of the four, he was still tiny. He was black all over, except for his white socks. Button looked up at Mandy and miaowed.

"He's lovely!" Mandy said happily, rubbing her cheek against the kitten's soft fur.

They played with the kittens for a while, and then they all went back on deck, and had tea and biscuits. As they were finishing their tea, Mr Hope turned to Lucy. "Mandy and James were saying you've been having problems with someone from the village."

Lucy quickly explained about Mr Pengelly. "We've only been here a little while," she said, "but he took against us from the start."

Mr Hope frowned. "I think Mr Pengelly's

being a little unfair," he said. He put out his hand, and scooped up the cat nearest to him. "Shall we start checking the cats over now? I think I recognise this one from Lucy's picture!"

"That's Queenie," said Mandy. "She's the one who brought us here!"

Mr Hope gave Queenie a quick check-up. "Well, you'll be glad to know that, apart from her leg, she seems to be very healthy. Now, who's next?"

Everyone helped to bring the cats to Mr and Mrs Hope to be checked over. But some of the cats didn't want to be checked over at all.

"Come out, Smokey!" gasped Martin. Some of the cats had gone below deck to hide, and Martin was flat on his tummy, trying to coax Smokey out from under one of the beds. "No one's going to hurt you."

Mandy came down from the deck to see what was going on. "I don't think she believes you!" she said. "Maybe you could get her out with some food?"

"Good idea," said Martin. "She loves cheese. I'll go and get some."

Martin managed to get Smokey out with a small piece of cheese. Almost all the cats had been checked over by now. Apart from Pusskin, whose sore eye Lucy had already noticed, the cats seemed to be in the best of health.

"Is that all of them?" Mandy asked. There were so many cats, it was impossible for her to keep count.

Lucy frowned. "I think there's just Jessie left. She's another of our nervous ones, and she's probably hidden herself away."

"What does she look like?" Mandy asked.

"She's black and white." Lucy smiled. "And she's easy to recognise, because she's much too fat!"

Mandy wandered round the deck, keeping a sharp look-out for Jessie. Then she spotted her. The small, round cat had wedged herself into a tiny gap between two lifebelts.

"Come on, Jessie," Mandy murmured gently. She knelt down and held out her

hand. But to her amazement, the cat put out its paw, and slapped her hand away.

Mandy jumped. She wasn't hurt, because the cat hadn't put its claws out. She was just surprised. She put out her hand again, and again the cat slapped it away.

Lucy saw what was happening, and came over. "Jessie used to belong to a family who teased her all the time," she said quietly, as she knelt down by Mandy. "And now, if she's scared, she hits out at people with her paw."

Mandy felt very upset. The cat looked so

unhappy. "Will she come out for you?" she asked.

"She might," Lucy replied. She knelt down, and, after a few minutes, she managed to get Jessie out to be checked over.

"Pusskin's eye infection should clear up in a couple of days, if you carry on bathing it," said Mr Hope, as he put his jacket back on. "It isn't serious."

"Thank you so much," said Lucy gratefully. "I was going to take him to the RSPCA clinic tomorrow, so you've saved me a trip."

"How long are you staying in the village?" Martin asked, as the Hopes and James got ready to leave.

"Until Sunday," said Mrs Hope. She looked at Mandy and James, who were saying goodbye to all the cats. "So I don't think you've seen the last of us!"

"Oh, please come and see us whenever you like!" said Lucy. "What about tomorrow morning?"

"We'd love to!" said Mandy eagerly.

They left the boat, waving to Lucy and

Martin and the cats, and began the walk back to the village.

Mandy couldn't stop thinking about Jessie and Smokey, who were so scared and unhappy. She turned to James. "We can't let Mr Pengelly force Lucy and Martin to abandon *The Puss-in-Boat*!"

"That's just what I was thinking!" James said. "But what can we do?"

"I don't know yet," said Mandy. Then she added, in her most determined voice, "But we'll have to think of something!"

4

A lost cat

Thursday morning was bright and sunny. Mandy and James were up early and, because it wasn't time for breakfast yet, they took Blackie out into the garden behind the hotel.

"I dreamt about cats all night!" James said with a grin.

"So did I!" said Mandy. "I can't wait to

go back to *The Puss-in-Boat* today."

"Me too," James agreed. Then he frowned. "I hope Mr Pengelly doesn't turn up though."

Mandy sighed. "I just wish he would give Lucy and Martin a chance," she said. "What on earth is going to happen to all the cats, if they have to leave the boat?"

James looked worried. "Have you come up with any brilliant ideas about how we can help them?"

Mandy shook her head. "Not really." Then she smiled. "But remember Tibby's six kittens? We found a good home for them, didn't we?"

James nodded, looking more cheerful. "Yes, we did!" But then his face fell again. "That was back home in Welford, though. It's different here. We don't know anybody."

Mandy knew what James meant. They couldn't just walk up to people they didn't know, and ask them if they wanted a cat. And, as Martin had said yesterday, older cats were a lot more difficult to find homes for than kittens. "We'll just have to do our very best," she said firmly.

"Yes, we will," James agreed. Then he looked round. "Oh no! Blackie! Stop that!" he shouted.

Blackie was having a lovely time digging a hole in one of the flowerbeds, and sending earth flying everywhere. James raced over, and dragged the puppy out.

"Bad dog, Blackie!" he gasped, pointing sternly at the Labrador. Blackie just wagged his tail, and jumped up to lick James's hand.

"Good morning, you two." Mrs Ross, the owner of the small bed–and–breakfast hotel, opened the door, and came out into the garden. She was a round woman with greying hair, and a warm smile. As soon as Blackie saw Mrs Ross, he pulled away from James and bounded up to her, wagging his tail. "And how's Blackie this morning?"

"Just as naughty as usual," said James. "I'm sorry, Mrs Ross, but he's dug a hole in one of your flowerbeds."

"Oh, don't worry about that," said Mrs Ross with a smile, as she bent down to

stroke the excited young dog. "It doesn't look like there's any serious damage done. Now, are you ready for breakfast?"

"Yes, please," James said eagerly.

"Well, why don't I give Blackie *his* breakfast, while you two go and wash your hands?" Mrs Ross suggested, with a twinkle in her eye. "I'm sure he's hungry after all that digging!"

"Thanks, Mrs Ross," James said gratefully, as she took Blackie indoors.

Mandy looked thoughtful as they washed their hands in the cloakroom. "I wonder what Mrs Ross thinks about *The Puss-in-Boat*," she said, as she reached for the soap. "Mr Pengelly said that no one in the village wants *The Puss-in-Boat* here. But perhaps some people don't feel like that. Mrs Cox, for instance: she asked Lucy to take in Effie, didn't she?"

"Yes," said James. "I bet Mrs Ross doesn't mind *The Puss-in-Boat*. She loves animals."

"There aren't many hotels that let you bring your pet on holiday with you," Mandy agreed.

James grinned. "Especially pets like Blackie!"

Mr and Mrs Hope were already sitting at the breakfast table in the dining-room, when Mandy and James hurried in.

"Hello, you two." Mrs Hope smiled at them. "Do you want cereal?"

"Yes, please," Mandy said. "We're starving!"

"What a surprise!" Mr Hope laughed as he passed James the cornflakes box. "So, I expect you two would like to go back to *The Puss-in-Boat* this morning, wouldn't you?"

Mandy nodded eagerly. "Lucy said we could."

"All right," Mrs Hope said, with a smile. "We'll take you there after we've finished breakfast. Your dad and I have decided to go for a long walk this morning."

Mrs Ross came in just then, carrying a large tray loaded with tea and toast. She brought it over to their table.

"Here we are, then." She beamed at them. "There's scrambled eggs, bacon and sausages coming in just a moment, and I've fed Blackie too. Goodness me, James, that dog of yours can eat!"

James grinned. "I know," he said. "Eating and misbehaving are Blackie's two favourite things!"

"So what are you all planning to do today then?" Mrs Ross asked, as she set out the teacups.

"James and I are going to *The Puss-in-Boat* to see Lucy and Martin and their cats," said Mandy. "Do you know them, Mrs Ross?"

"Yes, I do." Suddenly Mrs Ross looked

sad. "Lucy and Martin helped me to look for my cat when he went missing a few weeks ago. I don't know what I'd have done without them."

"I didn't know you had a cat, Mrs Ross," Mandy said.

"Poor William was too ill to make it home on his own," Mrs Ross sighed, looking even more upset. "He died a few days later. He was sixteen years old, so he'd had a good life. I miss him, though."

Mandy bit her lip. "I'm sorry, Mrs Ross."

Mrs Ross smiled at her a bit tearfully, and then began to bustle round the table, pouring out the tea. "Well, anyway, Lucy and young Martin seem very nice."

"They are," said James.

"They're doing a good job of looking after all those cats too," remarked Mr Hope. "But we've heard that some people in the village aren't happy about them being here."

Mrs Ross frowned. "That's true enough," she said. "There are some villagers who think that the cats are a nuisance, and that the boat's too small to have so many cats on it."

"It's very clean though," Mandy pointed out, "and so are the cats."

Mrs Ross nodded. "But I think some people are worried that Lucy might carry on taking in more and more strays. I suppose they're concerned that the village might be overrun with cats." She finished pouring out the tea. "Still, Lucy was very helpful to me. And I know for a fact that she looked after Miss Dawson's cat, when the old lady had to go into hospital for a few days."

Mandy was pleased. It looked like there were several people who wouldn't support Mr Pengelly. She wondered if Mrs Ross had heard about his threat to get rid of *The Puss-in-Boat*.

"Do you know Mr Pengelly, Mrs Ross?" she asked.

"Oh, yes, dear." Mrs Ross frowned. "I've heard he's not happy about *The Puss-in-Boat* at all."

"No, he isn't," said James. "We saw him there yesterday."

Mrs Ross shook her head. "I wouldn't

worry about Harry Pengelly," she said comfortingly. "He's not a bad person, but he's always got a bee in his bonnet about something. Now, I'd better get back to my kitchen, or there'll be no scrambled eggs for you today!"

Mandy frowned, as Mrs Ross went out. In spite of what the hotel owner had said, she was still worried. Mrs Ross might not take any notice of Mr Pengelly, but other people in the village might.

After breakfast, they all set off for *The Puss-in-Boat*. While Mandy and James were with Lucy and Martin, Mr and Mrs Hope were going to take Blackie with them on their country walk. The sun was getting warmer now, and there wasn't a cloud in the deep-blue sky.

Mandy and James ran eagerly on ahead, along the river-bank, with Blackie running beside them. They raced round the bend in the river. Lucy was standing on the deck of *The Puss-in-Boat*. They waved at her.

"We'll say a quick hello, and then we'll

be off," said Mr Hope, as he and Mrs Hope caught up.

They all went over to *The Puss-in-Boat*. Lucy was still on deck, but Mandy couldn't see Martin anywhere.

"Hello, Lucy," called Mrs Hope.

Lucy hurried across the deck of the barge towards them. "Hello, how lovely to see you all again."

"We're off on a walk," said Mr Hope. "We'll be back for Mandy and James in a couple of hours, if that's all right?"

"That's fine," said Lucy.

Mandy and James climbed on to *The Puss-in-Boat*.

"Bye then, you two," called Mrs Hope as she, Mr Hope and Blackie turned to leave. "Be good!"

"We will!" Mandy called back.

"Mum?" Martin suddenly appeared from below deck. He looked worried. "I can't find her. She isn't in the cabin." Then he saw Mandy and James. "Oh, hi there."

"Hello, Martin." Mandy looked puzzled. "Have you lost one of the cats?"

"It's Queenie," Martin said miserably. "We've looked all over the boat, and she isn't here."

"We haven't seen her since last night," Lucy added, looking worried. "She's never been gone this long before."

"We'll help you look for her, won't we, Mandy?" James offered.

"Of course we will," Mandy said. She couldn't bear to think of the little cat with its injured leg lost somewhere, cold and hungry. "Let's start right away!"

5

Looking for Queenie

"What about looking for Queenie along the river-bank?" Mandy suggested. "That's where James and I first saw her."

"Good idea," said Lucy. "If you, Martin and James go one way, I'll go the other."

They all climbed off the barge, and on to the river-bank.

"Now don't go too far," Lucy called

after them, as they set off.

Mandy, Martin and James walked slowly along, calling Queenie's name. They searched the hedgerows along the river-bank, but couldn't find Queenie anywhere. They went on until they had followed the path round the bend in the river.

"I think we'd better go back," Martin said.

Mandy stared along the river-bank. There was no sign of the little black cat anywhere. "Where can she be?" she asked miserably, as they started back towards the boat.

"You don't think she might have fallen into the river, do you?" asked James.

Martin shook his head. "Queenie hates the water. She won't go anywhere near it."

"All cats are like that, aren't they?" said James.

Martin smiled. "Not all of them," he said. "We used to have a cat called Victor who loved swimming!"

Mandy thought hard for a minute. "Do you think Queenie might have gone to the village?" she suggested.

"She might have done," Martin said.

"Let's go and see if Mum has had any luck."

They got back to *The Puss-in-Boat* just a few minutes before Lucy came hurrying towards them from the opposite direction. Mandy, James and Martin were waiting eagerly for her, but their faces fell when they saw that she was alone.

"Mandy suggested looking in the village, Mum," said Martin.

Lucy nodded. "It's a good idea. Let's go."

Lucy and Martin knew a footpath which took a short cut across the fields, and was much quicker than going by road.

The village was small and very pretty, with its old stone church and winding streets full of thatched cottages. They stopped by the churchyard, and Lucy turned to the others.

"I think we'd better split up again," she said. "I'll go this way." She pointed down the hill. "You three can look round the houses behind the church."

Mandy, James and Martin nodded.

"I'll meet you back here in ten minutes," Lucy called over her shoulder as she set off. "Don't be late!"

"Maybe we ought to look for Queenie in the churchyard too," Mandy suggested. "There are lots of places she could be hiding."

But Queenie wasn't in the churchyard.

Behind the church was a row of thatched cottages. All of the cottages had large front gardens filled with brightly-coloured flowers and shrubs. Mandy, James and Martin began to walk along the road, staring into all the gardens.

"I've just remembered who lives in one of these cottages," Martin said suddenly.

"Who?" asked James.

"Mr Pengelly!" Martin looked worried. "I hope Queenie isn't in his garden!"

Mandy frowned. "So do I!"

"Mr Pengelly said he'd found a cat from *The Puss-in-Boat* in his garden," James remembered. "But he didn't say which one."

"Which house is the Pengellys', Martin?" Mandy asked anxiously.

Martin pointed to the next house in the row. "Number Eight."

They stopped outside the gate, and glanced quickly round the front garden. Mandy felt very nervous indeed.

"I don't think Queenie's here," Martin said, sounding relieved.

"No," Mandy said. "Thank goodness!"

"Just a minute," James said suddenly. "Something just moved, over there in the flowerbed!"

Martin and Mandy looked where James was pointing, and Mandy's heart sank. There was Queenie, sitting under a large shrub, having a wash. After a few seconds, she started to settle down, looking as if she'd found the perfect spot for a nap.

"We've got to get her out," Mandy said desperately, "before Mr Pengelly sees her!"

"Queenie!" Martin called softly.

Queenie opened her big green eyes, and peered out through the leaves. She saw Martin and miaowed a greeting. Then she yawned, and closed her eyes again.

"Queenie!" Martin whispered again, but the cat took no notice.

"She's too sleepy to move," Mandy said

urgently. "We'll have to go and get her ourselves!"

Martin was already unlatching the gate. "I'll be as quick as I can," he whispered. "Let's hope no one sees us!"

He hurried into Mr Pengelly's garden, dashed over to the flowerbed, and scooped Queenie up into his arms. Queenie was surprised, but then she snuggled down on Martin's shoulder, and began to purr.

"Now get out of there!" Mandy said breathlessly.

But just then they heard the sound of a door opening. With sinking hearts, Mandy, James and Martin looked towards the house.

Mr Pengelly was standing on his doorstep, with a shopping bag in his hand, staring in amazement. "And just *what* do you think you're doing in my garden?"

6
Mandy's idea

For a moment or two, the three of them were too shocked to say anything. Then Mandy stepped forward. "We're very sorry, Mr Pengelly," she said in a wobbly voice. "We didn't mean any harm. Martin had to get his cat back, that's all."

Mr Pengelly looked at Queenie, and frowned. "That cat is always coming into my garden!" he said angrily. "I've had enough of this!"

"What on earth is going on?"

Everyone looked round. Lucy was hurrying towards them, looking worried.

"Mum!" Martin rushed over, and put Queenie into her arms. "We found Queenie in Mr Pengelly's garden."

"Yes, and I came out and found your son in here without my permission!" snapped Mr Pengelly.

"Oh dear!" said Lucy.

"Sorry, Mr Pengelly," said Martin.

The old man frowned. "This is just what I've been complaining about, Miss Browne!" he snapped. "That cat keeps coming into my garden, and digging up my flowerbeds—"

"She wasn't doing any harm," Martin argued. "She was just asleep."

Mr Pengelly looked even more annoyed. "That's all very well, but what if she starts encouraging your other cats to come and sleep in my garden? I'm not having it!"

Mandy got a sudden picture in her mind

of Queenie leading all the other cats from *The Puss-in-Boat* in a long line into Mr Pengelly's garden. It was such a funny thought that she wanted to laugh, but she didn't dare, because he looked so angry.

"I can't understand why Queenie would come into your garden, and no one else's," Lucy was saying. "No one else has complained."

"Well, what are you going to do about it?" Mr Pengelly folded his arms, and glared at them.

"We'll keep an eye on Queenie, and try

to make sure she doesn't go far from the boat," Lucy promised.

Mandy frowned. That wouldn't be easy. It was practically impossible to keep cats in one place, without locking them up.

Mr Pengelly shook his head. "I'm afraid that's not good enough, Miss Browne. I've decided to start a petition to get you and your boat moved on, and I'm going to get everyone in the village to sign it!"

"A petition!" Mandy gasped. She looked at Martin and James in horror. Things were going from bad to worse.

"Please, Mr Pengelly," said Lucy. "Can't we talk about this?"

"There's nothing to talk about," said the old man, and he marched off down the street.

"What an awful man!" said James indignantly.

Lucy sighed. "I don't think he's being very fair," she said. "But Queenie was in his garden, after all."

"How many people do you think will sign the petition, Lucy?" Mandy asked anxiously.

"I don't know," Lucy replied. "I haven't had any other complaints, so maybe he won't get many." But she didn't sound too sure.

"Mrs Ross won't sign it," said James.

"No, I'm sure she won't," Mandy agreed. But she was very worried about how many other people in the village would.

Lucy managed a smile. "Well, that's one person on our side, anyway! Come on, let's go back to *The Puss-in-Boat*."

They set off back to the barge.

"Shall I carry Queenie for a bit?" Mandy asked Lucy. "Your arms must be tired."

"Thanks, Mandy," Lucy replied gratefully. She gave Queenie to Mandy, and the little black cat settled herself down on Mandy's shoulder. She seemed to be enjoying the ride.

As she walked along, stroking Queenie's warm fur, Mandy thought hard about what she and James could do to help Lucy and Martin and the cats. They couldn't just let Mr Pengelly go ahead with his petition, and force *The Puss-in-Boat* to leave, or close down. They had to fight back. But how?

"Mandy?"

Mandy was thinking so hard that she didn't realise James was speaking to her. Then she blinked. "Sorry, James. What did you say?"

"Queenie's gone to sleep on your shoulder!" James grinned at her. "She must be tired out after all that excitement!"

Mandy gently hugged the little cat, and Queenie started to purr sleepily. "I was just thinking about Mr Pengelly," Mandy said. "If he's going to start a petition, then we have to do something too."

"But what?" asked Martin.

Mandy frowned. "I'm sure if everyone in the village knew the good job that *The Puss-in-Boat* was doing, they wouldn't sign the petition."

"Do people in the village know all about the cats?" James asked Lucy and Martin, as they walked along the river-bank.

Lucy shrugged. "Well, I suppose some of them do," she said. "I've helped a few people out when they needed their cats looking after or re-homed, but we don't know that many people in the village."

James looked at Martin. "Haven't you made any friends here yet?"

Martin shook his head. "We got here too late for me to start at the village school last term," he said. "I was going to go there after the holidays. But now it doesn't look like we'll be here . . ." His voice trailed away.

They were close to *The Puss-in-Boat* now. Penny and Pusskin, who were sitting on the river-bank, saw them, and came to meet them.

James knelt down to stroke the two cats. "It's such a shame," he sighed. "If only everyone in the village could come and see the cats and get to know them, I'm sure they wouldn't sign Mr Pengelly's petition."

Mandy gasped, and her face lit up. "James!" she said softly. "You're a genius!"

James looked puzzled. "I am?" he said, pushing his glasses up his nose.

"Lucy," Mandy said, her voice trembling

with excitement. "What about having an Open Day?"

"An Open Day?" Lucy repeated.

"Yes, so that everyone in the village can come along and visit *The Puss-in-Boat!*" Mandy explained breathlessly. "Then they can meet the cats, and see how well you look after them!"

"Oh, Mandy, what a brilliant idea!" said

Lucy, a huge smile spreading across her face.

Mandy turned pink. "Well, it was James's idea really," she pointed out.

"No, the Open Day was your idea, and I think it's great!" said James enthusiastically.

"So do I," Martin added.

Mandy looked pleased. "We can make some posters to advertise it," she said, thinking hard, "and put them up around the village. We want everyone to come."

"Even Mr and Mrs Pengelly?" asked James.

"*Especially* them!" Mandy said firmly. "And we could put out deckchairs and tables, and sell refreshments. What do you think, Lucy?"

Lucy nodded. "It's a good idea. But we can't have too many people on the barge at one time, though. There isn't room, and it wouldn't be safe."

"We could put the table and chairs on the river-bank, next to the barge," James suggested. "And we could decorate the boat with balloons and streamers."

"That would be lovely," Lucy agreed.

"And I could bake a few cakes and biscuits to sell."

"And we could sell cups of tea and coffee, and lemonade," James said eagerly.

"Maybe you could sell some of your paintings as well, Mum," Martin suggested.

"Why not?" Lucy agreed, as they all climbed aboard the barge. "We might even make some money for repairs!"

"Oh, I hope so!" said Mandy. Then, even if Lucy and Martin had to move on, at least they wouldn't have to give up the boat, and leave the cats behind.

"When shall we hold the Open Day?" asked Martin.

Lucy thought for a minute. "We'll have it on Saturday afternoon, the day before Mandy and James leave."

"But will we have enough time to get everything ready?" Mandy asked anxiously.

"Of course we will!" said Lucy. "Anyway, we can't have the Open Day without you two. After all, it was your idea!" She put her arm round Mandy's shoulder, which woke Queenie up. She opened her eyes, and miaowed grumpily.

"Don't worry, Queenie!" laughed Mandy. "You can be the star of the Open Day!"

"We'd better get started on some posters right away," said Lucy. "We need to let everyone in the village know about the Open Day, and we don't have much time."

Mandy nodded. She was determined to make the Open Day a big success. *The Puss-in-Boat* was depending on them.

Are you
CAT CRAZY?
Then why not
come to the
OPEN DAY
at
The Puss-In-Boot
This Saturday
at 2 o'clock.

7

An invitation

Mandy, James and Martin were sitting on the grassy river-bank, paper and paints spread out all around them.

"How are you getting on?" called Lucy. She was sitting on the deck of the barge, making a list of all the things they needed for Saturday afternoon.

Mandy held up her poster for Lucy to

see. "Open Day at *The Puss-In-Boat*!" it read in large, colourful letters, and she had drawn a black cat underneath the words. "That's supposed to be Queenie," she said, frowning at her drawing. "But I don't think it looks much like her!"

James and Martin were also hard at work. James's poster read:

Are you CAT CRAZY?
Then why not come to the Open Day
at *The Puss-in-Boat*?
This Saturday at 2 o'clock.

"I think I'll draw a picture of the barge at the bottom," James decided.

Martin had written the same words as James in the middle of his poster, and now he was drawing a border of cats all round the edge of the paper.

"Make sure the posters are really bold and bright!" Lucy called from the barge. "We've got to make people notice them!"

"Hello, everyone!"

They all looked round. Mr and Mrs Hope

and Blackie were walking along the river-bank towards them.

"Mum! Dad!" Mandy jumped to her feet, and raced to meet them. James and Martin followed her. Blackie saw them, and began to bark joyfully.

"Did you have a good walk?" James asked, as Blackie hurled himself into his arms.

"Yes, thank you, James," said Mr Hope.

"And what have you three been up to?" asked Mrs Hope curiously. She could see that Mandy, James and Martin were all nearly bursting with excitement.

Mandy explained about the Open Day.

"What a good idea!" said Mrs Hope. "We'll help, won't we, Adam?"

"Of course," said Mr Hope with a smile. "Just tell us what you want us to do."

"Thank you," said Lucy gratefully, as she climbed off the boat to join them. "But we don't want to spoil your holiday. And, anyway, there isn't much to do until Saturday."

"We're all going out tomorrow," said Mrs Hope.

Mandy suddenly remembered that the next day they were going to visit an old friend of her father's, Roger Thomas, who ran a wildlife hospital not far from Bilbury. She had been really looking forward to it, but with the excitement of the Open Day, she had forgotten all about it. Still, as Lucy had said, once the posters were up, there wasn't much more they could do until the actual afternoon of the Open Day arrived.

Lucy asked Mr and Mrs Hope on to the barge for a cup of tea, but they said no thank you, as they were dirty and muddy, and

really needed to go back to the bed and breakfast to change their clothes.

"I can drop Mandy and James off at the bed and breakfast when we've finished putting up the posters, if you like," Lucy suggested.

"Thank you," Mrs Hope said. "That would save us a trip back here to collect them."

"We'll see you all in an hour or two, then," called Mr Hope, as he and Mrs Hope carried on along the river-bank with Blackie.

Mandy, James and Martin continued with their posters, while Lucy went back to her list.

Mandy finished first. She rolled the poster up carefully, and put it with the others they had already made. They would have six posters to put up around the village. Soon everyone would know all about the Open Day.

Mandy wondered nervously how many villagers would actually come along. Mr Pengelly wouldn't, she thought, her heart sinking. But Mrs Ross had said that Mr

Pengelly wasn't a bad person. Maybe he would give *The Puss-in-Boat* another chance, if they could just make him see how important it was . . .

Mandy had an idea. She picked up a piece of paper, folded it in two to make a card and began to draw on the front of it.

"What are you doing?" asked Martin.

"Just wait and see," Mandy said mysteriously.

James and Martin looked at each other. "I think she's up to something," said James. "Mandy always has a scheme."

When the posters were finished, they all set off for the village to put them up. They stopped near the churchyard gate. Just to the side of the gate, there was a large noticeboard with a couple of posters, one about a village barn dance and another giving the times of the church services.

"I'll ask the vicar if I can put one on the noticeboard here," Lucy decided, taking three posters from Martin. "And one could go outside the school, and another outside the village hall."

"We could put one on the community noticeboard on the green," Martin suggested. "Lots of people would see it there."

"And we could ask Mrs Ross to put one in the window of the bed and breakfast," James added.

"Good idea," said Lucy. "Then we'll only have one left. Where can we put it?"

"I know!" Mandy said suddenly. "What about the post office? I'm sure Mrs Cox wouldn't mind. After all, you helped her out by taking Effie and her kittens in."

"That's a brilliant idea!" said Martin. "Lots of people go to the post office every day."

Lucy went to find the vicar. Meanwhile, Mandy, James and Martin walked on to the village green, and stopped at the community noticeboard. There wasn't anything on it except a poster about a mother and baby group at the church hall. Carefully Martin unrolled one of their posters, and pinned it in the middle of the board. They all stood back to admire it.

"Now the post office," said Martin.

"It's just across the green."

James and Martin set off across the grass, but the lace on one of Mandy's trainers had come undone, so she knelt down to re-tie it. As she did so, two women carrying shopping baskets stopped by the noticeboard.

"Look at that, Betty," said one of them, a short woman with dark hair. "There's an Open Day on Saturday, on that boat – the one with all the cats."

"You know I can't stand cats, Vera," said her friend. She was taller than the first woman, and wore large, horn-rimmed glasses. "Nasty, dirty creatures they are."

Mandy's heart sank as she tied up her lace. She hoped there weren't too many other people in the village who shared this view.

"I found my dustbin lid knocked off again this morning, and there was rubbish all over my garden path," Betty went on. "I bet it was those dratted cats."

"It could have been a fox, Betty," Vera pointed out quickly. "I quite like cats myself, you know. We used to have a lovely tabby

Are you
CAT CRAZY?
Then why
not come
to the
OPEN
DAY
at
The PUSS
-IN-BOOT
This Saturday
at 2 o'clock

called George years ago."

"I hear Harry Pengelly's getting up a petition to have that boat moved on," Betty remarked, as the two women walked on. "I've a jolly good mind to sign it."

"Oh, but I don't think they're doing any harm," Vera argued. "I might pop along to this Open Day myself, just to see what's going on . . ."

As Mandy ran to catch up with James and Martin, she couldn't help worrying about how many people in the village would agree with Mr Pengelly and Betty about the cats. They wouldn't know for sure, though, until the afternoon of the Open Day itself. It all depended on how many people bothered to turn up. Betty's friend hadn't sounded too sure about whether she was going to come or not. What if no one came at all?

Mandy decided not to tell James and Martin what the two women had said, as she caught up with them outside the post office. There was no point in them *all* worrying.

"Let's go and see Mrs Cox," said Martin.

They were about to go into the post office when the door opened and Mrs Ross came out.

"Hello, Mrs Ross," James said. "We were coming to see you later!"

Mrs Ross looked puzzled. "Whatever for?" she asked curiously.

Quickly Mandy explained about the Open Day. "And we were wondering if you would put up a poster in the window of the bed and breakfast," she finished.

Mrs Ross beamed at them. "What a wonderful idea!" she said. "And of course I'll put a poster up! But I hope you'll let me help out a little more than that."

"Yes, please!" said Mandy eagerly.

"Well, for one thing I have lots of deckchairs and garden tables you can borrow." Mrs Ross smiled at them. "I keep them for my guests, so I've got a lot more than most people."

"Thanks, Mrs Ross!" said James.

"And I could do a bit of baking for the refreshment stall," Mrs Ross added. "How about that?"

"That would be wonderful," said Martin gratefully.

"It's the least I can do after you and your mum helped me find my William," said Mrs Ross. She took one of the posters, and then hurried off down the road, turning back to wave at them.

"Isn't she nice?" said Mandy, as they went into the post office.

James nodded. "I hope she makes some of her raisin scones!" he said.

The post office was empty, except for Mrs Cox, who was sitting behind the counter, reading a magazine. She was a tall, thin woman, with an untidy bun of grey hair and round glasses.

"Hello, Martin," she said warmly. "How are you? And how are the kittens and their mum?"

"They're fine, Mrs Cox," said Martin.

"I'm glad to hear it," said the postmistress. "Now, what can I get for you and your friends?"

Martin gave her one of their posters. "We were wondering if you'd put this

up in your window," he said.

Mrs Cox unrolled the poster and looked at it. "Of course I will!" she said. "What a good idea! I'm sure lots of people in the village will come."

"We hope so," said Mandy.

The door opened and Lucy came in. "Hello, Mrs Cox," she said, then she turned to Mandy, Martin and James. "I've put all the posters up."

"So have we," said James.

"If you want to borrow any deckchairs, Lucy, I've got some in my garden," Mrs Cox offered, "and I can let you have some paper plates and plastic cups."

"Oh, thank you, Mrs Cox!" said Lucy gratefully.

"Mrs Ross is lending us some chairs and tables too," said Mandy, "and she's going to bake some refreshments."

"Everyone's being so kind," said Lucy. "I just hope the cats appreciate it!"

"Of course they will!" said Mandy.

"Martin and I will walk you two back to the bed and breakfast now," said Lucy, glancing at her watch. "Come on."

They said goodbye to Mrs Cox and went out. Mandy was feeling quite cheerful again now. As Lucy had pointed out, most people were being very helpful about the Open Day. Mandy was beginning to think that it couldn't possibly fail . . .

But there was a nasty shock waiting for them outside the post office. Mr Pengelly was standing there, holding a clipboard, and talking to a large man who wore a flat cap.

". . . and this petition is to try and get that boatful of cats moved on," Mr Pengelly was saying, as he showed the man the papers he was holding. "As you can see, I've got some signatures already."

Mandy was horrified. Mr Pengelly hadn't wasted any time starting up his petition. How many signatures had he got already? A lot or just a few? As they walked by, Mandy tried to sneak a look at the clipboard he was holding, but she couldn't see. Mr Pengelly didn't notice them going by. He was too busy talking to the man in the flat cap.

"I'll sign it," Mandy heard the man say as they walked on. "My dustbin lid was knocked off again this morning, and there was rubbish all over my lawn. I'm fed up with it."

"It's not fair!" Mandy burst out as soon as they were out of earshot. "It could easily be a fox that's raiding the dustbins!"

Lucy nodded. "Maybe we could ask if anyone in the village has seen foxes around at night."

"I wonder how many people have signed

Mr Pengelly's petition," James said anxiously.

Nobody answered, but everyone looked miserable. Then Mandy remembered the card she had made when they were designing the posters. She had slipped it into her pocket, and forgotten about it. "Before we go to the bed and breakfast, can we go to Mr Pengelly's house?" she asked Lucy.

"Mr *Pengelly's* house?" Martin and James said together, staring at Mandy in amazement. Lucy looked surprised too.

Mandy took a deep breath. She was feeling a bit silly now, but it was too late to get out of it. So she took the card she had made out of her pocket.

"I've made a special invitation for Mr and Mrs Pengelly," she explained. "I thought that maybe then they might come to the Open Day."

James looked doubtful. "I don't think they will."

Martin shook his head. "Me neither."

"Well, at least they can't say they haven't been invited!" Mandy said stubbornly.

"I think it's a very nice thought," Lucy agreed.

They walked to Mr Pengelly's house. While the others waited at the gate, Mandy went up the path, and pushed the invitation through the letterbox. Then, as she turned to leave, she noticed something very odd indeed. There was a dustbin near the front door. The bin was very full, so the lid didn't fit properly, and through the gap, Mandy could see what looked like the edge of an empty cat food tin.

Cat food? Mandy frowned. The Pengellys didn't have a cat. So why was there an empty cat food tin in their dustbin?

8

Helping out

"Well," said Mr Hope as he turned the Land-rover down the road that led back to Bilbury, "I think we all enjoyed that!"

"I did!" said Mandy eagerly. "The fox cubs were gorgeous!"

It was the following afternoon, and the Hopes and James had just returned from visiting Roger Thomas, Mr Hope's friend.

They had set out after breakfast, and had soon arrived at the wildlife hospital, which wasn't far away. The hospital was a long bungalow with large grounds in the middle of the countryside.

As soon as Mr Hope pulled up outside the building, Roger Thomas, a cheery-looking man with dark hair, came out to meet them.

"Adam! Emily!" he called. "Great to see you!" Roger welcomed Mandy and James too. "I've heard you both quite like animals?" he went on, with a twinkle in his eyes.

"We *love* animals!" said Mandy eagerly. She could hardly wait to see what kind of animals were being cared for at the hospital.

"Then you've come to the right place!" said Roger. "Come on, I'll give you the guided tour."

The hospital was looking after all sorts of sick wild animals. There was a young deer with a broken leg, two owls with injured wings, and several hedgehogs amongst the many patients. There were also two fox cubs, who had lost their mother.

Mandy gave a gasp of delight when she saw them. "They're gorgeous!" she said softly, stroking their russet-coloured heads.

"They're due for a feed soon," Roger told her. "You can help the nurse give them their milk if you like."

Mandy and James were thrilled. Roger gave each of them a cub to hold while the nurse fetched the bottles of milk. The cubs were lively and inquisitive, and one of them even tried to go head first down James's sweatshirt. But as soon as the milk arrived the cubs settled down for their feed.

"It's a bit like feeding a baby!" Mandy laughed, as the cubs drained their bottles right down to the last drop.

After helping to feed the fox cubs Mandy and James joined Roger and Mr and Mrs Hope for a delicious lunch, before heading back to Bilbury.

Mandy had been so interested in the wildlife hospital and its patients, especially the fox cubs, that she had forgotten about *The Puss-in-Boat* for a little while. But now, as they drove into the village, she started wondering what had been happening while they had been away. Had Mr Pengelly been out collecting more signatures for his petition?

"Look!" said James suddenly. "There are Lucy and Martin!"

Lucy and Martin were walking up the high street, carrying bags of shopping. Mr Hope tooted the horn, and then pulled into the kerb.

"Hello," called Mrs Hope, winding down the window. "How are you both?"

"All right, thank you," said Lucy, although Mandy thought both she and Martin looked a bit depressed. "We've been to buy decorations and drinks for tomorrow."

"And we met Mr Pengelly," Martin added. "You'll never guess what he's done!"

"What?" asked Mandy.

"He's called a meeting in the village hall on Monday night to discuss *The Puss-in-Boat*!" Lucy told them worriedly.

"Oh no!" Mandy exclaimed.

"At least Mr Pengelly's meeting is after

the Open Day," James said. "Maybe by then we'll have enough people on our side."

"I hope so," Lucy sighed. Then she looked up at the sky, and groaned. "Oh, no, it's starting to rain! That's all we need!"

Mandy's heart sank as big drops of rain began to splash on to the Land-rover's windscreen. Who would bother to come to the Open Day in weather like this?

"Can we give you a lift?" asked Mr Hope.

Lucy shook her head. "Thanks, but we've got more shopping to do."

"We'll see you tomorrow morning then," said Mrs Hope.

They waved goodbye to Lucy and Martin, and Mr Hope drove on. Mandy gazed miserably up at the grey sky as the rain grew heavier. At this rate, it looked as if the Open Day was doomed before it had even started!

9
Open Day

As soon as Mandy opened her eyes on Saturday morning, she jumped out of bed, and hurried over to the window. She pulled the curtains back, and looked eagerly outside. Her face fell. The sky was grey and overcast. Still, at least it wasn't raining, she thought, trying to be cheerful.

The Open Day was scheduled to start at

two o'clock, and there was a lot of work to be done before then. After breakfast, Mandy and James helped Mr and Mrs Hope pack the Land-rover with deckchairs and tables. Mrs Cox had given them a big silver urn to boil water for tea and coffee, as well as packets of plastic cups and cutlery, and paper plates.

"At least that means there won't be any washing-up to do when the Open Day's over!" Mrs Hope said, looking relieved.

At last everything was packed tightly in, and Mr Hope closed the doors. "We'll see you at *The Puss-in-Boat*!" he called, and drove off with Mrs Hope. Mandy and James had promised to help Mrs Ross pack up and deliver the cakes she had baked for the Open Day, so they hurried back into the bed and breakfast to find her.

"I can't wait for it to start," James said eagerly as they went towards the kitchen.

"Me too." But Mandy couldn't help sounding a bit worried, and James frowned. "Are you all right, Mandy?" he asked.

Mandy nodded. "It's just – well, what if no one turns up?"

"Of course people will turn up," James said confidently. "No one would miss out on a great day like this!"

Mandy managed a smile. "I suppose not," she said, as she knocked at the kitchen door.

"Come in," Mrs Ross called.

Mandy and James opened the door, and walked in. Their eyes grew wide with amazement. Lined up on the kitchen counter were four large, delicious-looking cakes, along with three plates piled with scones and biscuits, and a plate of jam tarts.

"Do you think that will be enough?" Mrs Ross asked. "I didn't have time to make any more."

"Mrs Ross, it's brilliant!" Mandy said, her eyes shining. Then she looked more closely at the plate of gingerbread biscuits, and began to laugh. "Oh, James, look!"

Instead of gingerbread men, Mrs Ross had made gingerbread cats, with curly tails and currants for eyes. Mandy and James were thrilled.

"I've had that cat-shaped biscuit cutter for years and never used it," Mrs Ross said, beaming at them. "I thought today was the *purr*-fect time to try it out!"

Mandy and James groaned at the joke. They helped Mrs Ross pack the cakes carefully into boxes, then they set off to walk to *The Puss-in-Boat*.

As they passed the poster they had stuck up on the community noticeboard, Mandy wondered again how many people had seen the posters and decided to come along. Well, she wouldn't have to wait long to find out.

They turned down into the road where the Pengellys lived.

"I hope we don't meet Mr Pengelly!" James whispered in Mandy's ear. But there was no one around except for a milkman, standing next to his milk float, talking to a woman. It wasn't until they got closer that Mandy saw it was Mrs Pengelly.

"And I'll have an extra pint of milk, please," Mrs Pengelly was saying.

The milkman smiled. "That makes three extra pints this week!" he said. "Someone's drinking a lot of milk in your house!"

He took three bottles from the float, and handed them to Mrs Pengelly, who hurried back into the cottage.

"Do you know Mrs Pengelly?" Mandy asked Mrs Ross.

"Not very well," Mrs Ross replied. "She keeps herself to herself. She doesn't say much."

"Mr Pengelly doesn't give anyone a chance to say anything!" James pointed out.

Mrs Ross smiled. "Well, let's hope he calms down a bit and comes to the Open Day," she said.

They took the short cut to the river across the fields. As they got closer to the barge, they could see that everyone was busy. Mr Hope was setting out the tables and chairs on the river-bank, Mrs Hope and Lucy were standing on stepladders hanging streamers and balloons in the trees, and Martin was unpacking the plastic cups.

James went to help Martin, and Mrs Ross and Mandy began to set up the refreshments stall.

"Mrs Ross, you're a marvel!" Lucy exclaimed, as they unpacked all the cakes, biscuits and scones. "Thank you so much for doing all this."

"It's a pleasure," said Mrs Ross. "After all, you helped me when I needed it."

Mandy tried not to keep worrying, but she couldn't help it. Would it rain? The sky still looked grey, although it was a little brighter than when she had woken up that morning. What if Mr Pengelly had already turned most of the villagers against the barge?

Mandy hoped desperately that the Open Day would be a success. She couldn't bear to think what would happen to *The Puss-in-Boat*'s cats if it wasn't.

It was almost two o'clock. In a few minutes the Open Day was due to start, and Mandy stood on the river-bank, looking round. The boat looked wonderful with its balloons and streamers, and with Lucy's cat paintings displayed all over the cabin. The nearby trees were decorated too. Some of the cats were

lying around on the boat deck, and some were strolling on the river-bank, weaving their way between the tables and chairs. Mandy looked for Queenie, but couldn't see her.

Mrs Ross was behind the refreshments stall, which was laden with the cakes, scones and biscuits that she and Lucy had baked. The hot water urn was steaming gently, ready for making tea and coffee, and bottles of lemonade were lined up next to the piles of plastic cups. Everything was ready.

"I think we're all set!" Lucy smiled. She put her arm round Mandy's shoulders. "Now all we've got to do is wait for people to turn up!"

Mandy smiled back, even though her heart was pounding. Then, suddenly, James grabbed her arm.

"Look!" he said.

Mandy looked where James was pointing. There was a man, a woman and a little girl walking across the fields towards *The Puss-in-Boat*. Her face lit up. "Are they coming here?"

"It looks like it," Mr Hope said. "We'd better start opening those bottles of lemonade!"

An hour or so later, Mandy couldn't even remember why she'd been so worried. There had been just a few visitors at first, and then more and more had arrived. Now the Open Day was in full swing.

Although the sky was still overcast, it hadn't rained, and now and then a gleam of pale sunshine broke through. There were people sitting around on the river-bank, chatting, drinking tea and lemonade and eating Mrs Ross's and Lucy's cakes.

Some of the visitors were holding cats in their arms or on their laps. Mandy spotted Pusskin being petted by one man, and Penny in the arms of a little girl. Meanwhile, Mandy's parents were busy answering questions about pet care, and especially about looking after cats. James and Martin had made a big sign reading "ASK THE VET", and there was a long line of people queuing to speak to Mr and Mrs Hope.

Lucy was on the deck of *The Puss-in-Boat*, and people were going on board to see for themselves where the cats lived, as well as to look at Lucy's paintings. Mandy could see that she'd already sold a few of them.

The only thing that wasn't so good was that Mr and Mrs Pengelly hadn't come, after all. Mandy sighed. She hadn't really thought that her invitation would do the trick, but she couldn't help hoping . . .

"Mandy!" Lucy hurried over to her. "Isn't this wonderful? Everything's going so well!"

Mandy grinned at her.

"I've sold four cat paintings," Lucy went on, "and two other people have asked me if I can do a portrait of their pets."

"That's great!" Mandy said happily.

"But best of all, I think I might have found new homes for some of the cats!" Lucy beamed at her. "I've got homes for all the kittens, as soon as they're old enough. Someone has asked me about adopting Lily, and another lady wants Muffin. Oh, and Mrs Ross is having Pusskin!"

That was the best news of all! To know

that some of the cats would be going to loving homes was the best reward for all their hard work.

"Goodness me!" Lucy said suddenly, sounding very surprised. "Here come Mr and Mrs Pengelly! I never expected to see them!"

Mandy's face lit up. Mr and Mrs Pengelly had come to the Open Day! Maybe her special invitation had done the trick after all! But when she looked over at the

Pengellys, she wasn't so sure. Mr Pengelly was marching along the river-bank with a large cardboard box in his arms, looking very red in the face. Mrs Pengelly was hurrying along behind him, and she looked rather red too.

Mandy felt her heart sink. The Open Day had been going so well. Had Mr and Mrs Pengelly come to spoil it?

10

A confession

Just at that moment, Mr Pengelly spotted Lucy and Mandy. He headed straight towards them, looking very angry indeed. Mrs Pengelly scurried along behind him.

"Hello, Mr Pengelly," Lucy said nervously. "We're so glad you decided to come to the Open Day—"

"We're not here for the Open Day!"

snapped Mr Pengelly. "We're here to return this!"

He pulled open the box he was holding, and Queenie stuck her head out. She saw Lucy and Mandy and began to miaow loudly. Mandy bit her lip. It looked like the little cat had been caught in Mr Pengelly's garden once again.

"Oh, Queenie!" Lucy sighed, lifting the cat out of the box. "Why can't you behave yourself?"

"I found her under my rosebush," Mr Pengelly went on furiously. "And I want to know what you're going to do about it!"

Lucy looked helplessly at him. "I just don't know why Queenie keeps on going into your garden, Mr Pengelly. I'm very sorry."

"That's not good enough!" snapped Mr Pengelly. "And I'm not standing for it any longer!"

Mandy glanced at Mrs Pengelly to see what she thought. But Mrs Pengelly didn't look angry, she looked very embarrassed. Maybe she was just ashamed of Mr Pengelly for making a scene at the Open Day. Unless there was another reason . . .

Mandy remembered the empty tin of cat food she had seen in the Pengellys' dustbin, as well as the extra pints of milk Mrs Pengelly had bought from the milkman.

"Excuse me, Mr Pengelly," she said slowly. "I think I might know why Queenie keeps coming to your garden."

Mr Pengelly stared at Mandy. "What do you mean?"

"Well," Mandy looked at Mrs Pengelly. "Cats keep going back to a place if someone there is feeding them."

Mrs Pengelly turned bright red.

"No one's feeding that cat at *my* house!" Mr Pengelly began crossly, but then his wife cleared her throat.

"Er – Harry," she said quietly, "I think it's time for me to own up."

Mr Pengelly turned to stare at his wife.

"I've been feeding Queenie," Mrs Pengelly said.

"*You*?" spluttered Mr Pengelly. "But why?"

Mrs Pengelly smiled at her husband.

"Because she reminds me of our Sooty," she said.

"Who's Sooty?" Mandy asked.

"The cat we had when we were first married," Mrs Pengelly replied. She tickled Queenie under the chin. "You remember our Sooty, don't you, Harry?"

Mr Pengelly stared hard at Queenie. "I suppose she does look a bit like Sooty," he muttered reluctantly.

"Sooty was such a lovely cat!" Mrs Pengelly went on. "Do you remember how he sat on your lap for hours in the evenings? He was so fond of you, Harry!"

Mr Pengelly didn't say anything, but Mandy thought she saw him almost smile, even though he still looked embarrassed.

"We used to say that Sooty was the most handsome cat in town!" Mrs Pengelly smiled at her husband. "Well, Queenie's just as beautiful."

She put out her hand, and gently stroked Queenie's head. The cat purred, and climbed into her arms. "I'm sorry, Miss Browne." Mrs Pengelly looked nervously at Lucy. "I thought Queenie was a stray when I started feeding her. I've been feeling very guilty about getting you into trouble."

"That's all right." Lucy smiled at her. "I'm glad we've got this sorted out!"

Mandy looked at Mr Pengelly. He didn't look angry any more, just very embarrassed. Mandy couldn't help feeling a bit sorry for him.

"I'm sorry, Miss Browne," he muttered. "Obviously I didn't know that my wife was – er – encouraging the cat to come into our garden."

"Won't you both come and have some tea?" Lucy asked. "Then you can see how careful we are to look after the cats properly."

But Mr Pengelly shook his head. "I've got to get back home," he muttered. "Got some jobs to do in the garden."

"I'll stay for a little while," said Mrs Pengelly. "I'd like a cup of tea. And then I'd like to have a look around *The Puss-in-Boat*, if I may."

Mr Pengelly hurried off, while his wife went over to the refreshments stall, still carrying Queenie in her arms.

Her eyes shining with relief, Lucy turned to Mandy, and patted her on the back. "Well done! How on earth did you work out that Mrs Pengelly was feeding Queenie?"

Mandy explained about the extra milk Mrs Pengelly was having delivered, and the cat food tin in the dustbin. "But I didn't guess what they meant until I saw how embarrassed Mrs Pengelly looked," she said.

"Well, let's hope that this will stop Mr Pengelly from causing further trouble for *The Puss-in-Boat*!" Lucy said happily.

James and Martin came running over, Blackie at their heels. "What did Mr Pengelly want?" asked James.

Lucy smiled at the two boys. "We'll tell you all about it," she said. "But first let's go over to the refreshments stall, because Mandy deserves a big slice of chocolate cake!"

Mandy turned pink with pleasure. The Open Day was turning out to be a success. Maybe now Mr Pengelly might drop his petition against *The Puss-in-Boat*, and cancel the meeting at the village hall. Then Lucy and Martin and the cats would be able to stay.

Mandy smiled as they went over to the refreshments stall. The Open Day had been hard work, but it had all been worth it to try to keep the cats safe.

The Open Day was so popular, it continued into the early evening. As soon as the last visitor had left, the Hopes, James, Lucy, Martin and Mrs Ross set to work tidying up, packing away the chairs and tables and picking up the litter. It was hard work, and they didn't finish until quite late.

"I think the Open Day has been the best part of the whole holiday!" James said with an enormous yawn.

"Well, I for one have never worked quite so hard on a holiday before!" Mr Hope replied with a smile. "But it was definitely worth it."

"We've raised such a lot of money!" Lucy said happily. "I think we'll be able to start having the barge repaired quite soon!"

Mandy was delighted. That meant that even if Lucy and Martin did have to move on, at least they wouldn't have to leave the boat and the cats behind. If only Mr Pengelly would stop his campaign to get *The Puss-in-Boat* moved on, everything would be perfect. They would just have to wait and see what the old man decided to do next.

"I can't believe we're going home today!" Mandy sighed, as she, James, Mr and Mrs Hope and Blackie walked along the river-bank. "I'm really going to miss *The Puss-in-Boat*."

Mrs Hope put her arm round Mandy. "We all will," she said. "But at least we've done our very best to help."

Mandy nodded. It was Sunday morning, the day after the Open Day, and they were on their way to say goodbye to Lucy, Martin and the cats before they went back home to Welford.

When they arrived at *The Puss-in-Boat*, Martin was on the deck, feeding some of the cats. Lucy was down in the cabin, but she hurried out when they climbed aboard, Mr Hope carrying Blackie.

"Hello," Lucy called. "Are you ready to leave?"

"We'll be going in about an hour," said Mrs Hope.

"And how's Pusskin settling in at the bed and breakfast?" asked Lucy.

"He loves it," Mandy replied. "He and Mrs Ross are great friends already."

Martin came over to them, carrying Queenie. "There's someone here who wants to say goodbye to you," he said, and he put the black cat into Mandy's arms.

"Hello, Queenie!" said Mandy, stroking the cat's head, "I'm going to miss you!"

"Me too," said James. "After all, she was the one who brought us here."

"She's a very clever cat!" said Martin, tickling Queenie under the chin.

Mandy noticed a man coming across the fields towards the barge. She recognised him, and frowned. "That's Mr Pengelly!" she said.

Lucy looked nervous. "Oh dear!" she said. "What does he want now?"

They all waited in silence as Mr Pengelly came up to the barge. Mandy's heart was in her mouth. Surely Mr Pengelly hadn't come to complain about something else?

Looking embarrassed, Mr Pengelly nodded a good morning to everyone. Then he looked at Lucy. "I'd like a word with you, Miss Browne, if I may."

"Yes, of course," Lucy said, "Do come on board."

Mr Pengelly climbed carefully on to the deck. "My wife and I had a long talk yesterday, and . . ." Mr Pengelly stopped and cleared his throat, ". . . she tells me that your boat is very clean and tidy." He glanced round the deck. "And I can see for myself that she's right."

Lucy smiled. "Thank you."

"I want you to know that I've called off my – er – campaign to have you and your cats moved on," Mr Pengelly muttered. "I won't be going ahead with the petition or the meeting."

Mandy and James grinned at each other. *The Puss-in-Boat* was safe!

119

"There's just one more thing." Mr Pengelly looked even more embarrassed. "My wife's very upset at the thought of Queenie not coming round any more." He looked at Queenie, who was still in Mandy's arms. "So I was wondering if we could – er – keep her?"

Mandy could hardly believe her ears. "You mean you want to adopt her?"

Mr Pengelly nodded. "If that's all right?" He looked at Lucy.

"Perfectly all right!" said Lucy cheerfully. "I think you and Mrs Pengelly will give Queenie a wonderful home! We'll bring her round to you later on today, if you like."

Mr Pengelly nodded, turning even redder. He said a hasty thank you and goodbye, patted Queenie quickly on the head and hurried away.

"Well!" said James. "Mrs Ross said Mr Pengelly wasn't a bad person, and she was right!"

"That's four cats who have found homes now, as well as all the kittens," Mandy said.

"Five," said Martin. "The vicar came to

see us this morning. He wants to adopt Penny. He's got mice in the vicarage!"

"I'm so glad we can stay!" Lucy said joyfully. "We've made some good friends here, and Martin will be able to go to the village school."

Mandy grinned. Even she could hardly believe how well things had turned out.

"Time for us to be going," said Mr Hope, glancing at his watch.

"Goodbye, Queenie," said Mandy, and she gave the cat a final hug.

"Goodbye, Queenie," said James, doing the same. "We won't forget you!"

"And we won't forget you!" said Lucy. "These are just to say thank you for all your help!" She held up two small water-colour pictures of a black cat, and gave one each to Mandy and James.

"It's Queenie!" James said. "Thanks!"

"Thank you very much!" Mandy added, her eyes shining with delight. The paintings would be the perfect reminder of a *purr*-fect summer holiday!